*This book is dedicated with love to
my daughter Felicity and
my God-daughters Emma Louise Cassidy
and Laura Marie Cassidy.*

The Terrible Trials of
Mattie McCrum

Janey Preger
Illustrated by Lorraine White

A & C Black · London

The Crackers Series

Calamity Kate	Terry Deary
The Custard Kid	Terry Deary
Eating Ice Cream with a Werewolf	Phyllis Green
Fatbag	Jeremy Strong
Fox on the Roof	Jeremy Strong
Hoods and Heroes	Nick Warburton
Karate Princess	Jeremy Strong
The Lambton Worm	Terry Deary
Lightning Lucy	Jeremy Strong
Lightning Lucy Strikes Again	Jeremy Strong
Money Doesn't Grow on Trees	Jeremy Strong
Starbiker	Jeremy Strong
The Terrible Trials of Mattie McCrum	Janey Preger
Trouble with Animals	Jeremy Strong
Windmill of Nowhere	Terry Deary
The Wishing Well Ghost	Terry Deary
The Woff	Jeremy Strong

First published 1987 by A & C Black (Publishers) Ltd.,
35 Bedford Row, London WC1R 4JH.

British Library Cataloguing in Publication Data
Preger, Janey
   The terrible trials of Mattie McCrum.—
   (The Crackers series)
   I. Title II. White, Lorraine III. Series
   823'.914 [J] PZ7

ISBN 0–7136–2881–2

Filmset by August Filmsetting, Haydock, St Helens
Printed in Great Britain by R J Acford Ltd., Chichester.

I

Mattie is bored

It was a Saturday afternoon and Mattie McCrum was staring out of her bedroom window. She was watching Stanley, her cat, chasing a bee. Stanley was rather fat so he wasn't doing very well. Mattie waved to him. Then she sighed deeply.

'I think I'm the most bored person in the history of the world,' she muttered to herself. 'My room is boring, my hair is boring, my feet are boring and so are my teeth. In fact, my whole life is boring.'

Mattie did not get on well with the sort of girls who had masses of hobbies and never had a spare moment. She liked reading, drawing, eating, listening to music, making jokes and day-dreaming.

She dreamed about being a famous ice skater, a star ballerina, a brilliant gymnast and a best-selling author. She thought she would make a good explorer if only someone would give her the chance.

'Well, sitting on your bottom won't turn you into a famous explorer,' her mother said.

Her father laughed. 'You could win a cup for eating,' he told her, after he had watched her eat four apples and three packets of crisps.

Mattie felt misunderstood.

She gazed out of the window for a bit. Then

suddenly she had an idea. She went to find her father who was washing up in the kitchen and dreaming about being a famous cricketer. At least Mr McCrum played cricket as well as just thinking about it.

'Shot . . . sir,' yelled the crowd, as Mr McCrum bowed and smiled. Mattie walked in.

'I'm the most bored person in the history of the world,' she said.

'Hang on,' said her father. 'I'm just bowling out the bank manager.' He stood at the sink for a moment then he turned to Mattie and said, 'I already know that. Tell me something new.'

Mattie told him that she thought it would fill up her spare time wonderfully if she could go and stay

with a different relative each weekend. Mr McCrum looked puzzled.

'Why on earth would you want to do that?' he asked her. 'Most of our relatives are awful.'

'Yes. But I could stand them for a weekend,' said Mattie.

'But could they stand you?' he said.

Mrs McCrum joined in the discussion and they decided to give it a try. It was arranged that Mattie would go to stay with her Auntie Kim and cousin Samantha the next Saturday.

'I'd better warn you,' said Mrs McCrum. 'You might hate it.'

But Mattie was sure she would have a lovely time.

Mattie and the Little Gems

Mattie walked up the stairs until she came to the second floor. A large white and gold sign said:

MADAME WANDA
FAMOUS STAGE SCHOOL
TV APPEARANCES
PANTOMIME
TAP · DRAMA · BALLET

Mattie did not know why Auntie Kim had changed her name to 'Madame Wanda', but she supposed it was because 'Auntie Kim' didn't sound important enough. She pressed the bell.

Through the door Mattie could hear piano music and Auntie Kim shouting:

'And ONE and TWO and THREE and KICK and ONE and TWO and THREE and JUMP ... No, no Marlon, I said JUMP not KICK.'

The door opened and there was Samantha, Auntie Kim's daughter. She was wearing a pink sweat-shirt with a big sparkly letter 'S' on the front, pink sneakers and a pink skirt with a big 'S' on the pocket.

Mattie was wearing faded jeans, old gym shoes and a red jersey that didn't have a big sparkly 'M' on the front.

'Oh hi,' said Samantha in a bored voice. 'It's you.'

Mattie felt like saying 'No it's not, it's next door's dog,' but Samantha wasn't a very jokey sort of girl, so she didn't.

They went into a big hall where lots of children in leotards were jumping about and trying to keep time with the music. Auntie Kim was standing on a small platform, looking cross. She had red curls piled on top of her head and wore a red and black dress. In her hand was a wooden stick, and every time anyone did something wrong, which seemed to be very often, Auntie Kim would reach out and prod them with it.

Miss Mims was playing the piano. She was quite old and always looked on the verge of tears. She reminded Mattie of a water vole.

'No Marlon,' bawled Auntie Kim, 'You're suppose to be a sunflower!' which made Mattie laugh because anyone less like a sunflower than Marlon would be hard to imagine. He was fat with black curls, and red cheeks, and ears that stuck out.

Auntie Kim waved graciously, as though she were the Queen and Mattie one of her loyal subjects, so Mattie waved graciously back, and then followed Samantha through to the flat at the back of the hall where they lived.

It was a nice modern flat. 'Modern', thought Mattie, was Auntie Kim's favourite word. In fact you could hardly get in the nice modern kitchen for all Auntie Kim's modern gadgets – the blender, the mixer, the electric fan, the coffee-maker, the enormous freezer and the microwave oven.

'I've got a new bed,' boasted Samantha. 'It's a brass four-poster with lace curtains and an embroidered pillow.'

'With 'S' for Samantha I suppose?' said Mattie.

'Yes,' said Samantha. 'How did *you* know?'

Mattie wanted to say, 'Because you always have 'S' on everything. I wouldn't be surprised if you had 'S' on your tummy, in nice sparkly writing of course.' But she didn't. She remembered that she had begged to come and she must try to enjoy herself.

'Can you tap dance?' asked Samantha.

Mattie couldn't really dance at all, but she was feeling fed up about Samantha's new bed, so instead of saying 'No' as she should have done, she said, 'Yes, and I've won a cup for it. A silver trophy.'

'Coo,' said Samantha. 'I didn't know that. It could come in very handy.'

'Oh dear,' thought Mattie. 'What does she mean?' But she felt too nervous to ask.

Samantha took Mattie to see the new bed. It was very pretty.

'Look at this,' said Samantha. She opened a
drawer and took out a velvet box. Inside was a gold
bracelet in the shape of a snake. It had two green
jewels for eyes and a little green jewel in its tail.

'I won it for dancing at the old people's party,'
said Samantha. 'They said I danced like
thistledown.'

'In the shape of an 'S' I suppose,' thought
Mattie, but she said. 'How nice. It's lovely.'

'I must go and tell Mum about you being able
to tap dance,' Samantha said. 'She's short of a
Little Gem for the gala performance.'

The Little Gems were Auntie Kim's famous
dancing troupe of boys and girls. Mattie didn't like
them at all.

'One of the Little Gems has got measles,' said
Samantha. 'Mum'll be ever so pleased.'

9

'Can't she manage without the extra Gem?' asked Mattie worriedly.

'Of course not,' laughed Samantha. 'It spoils the whole chorus line and set piece. She's been going mad. Really mad!'

'Oh,' said Mattie in a small voice. She thought 'I'll have to tell her I can't dance,' but then she'd feel silly and could just imagine Samantha's big nose and her big blue eyes looking all snooty and important. So she said nothing. 'If there's one thing on earth I don't want to be,' she thought to herself, 'it's a Little Gem. I'd rather be a lion tamer. I'd rather eat a spider sandwich. I'd rather do sums for the rest of my life.'

Samantha gave Mattie a chocolate milk-shake and a biscuit in the shape of a parrot, then she went to find Auntie Kim. That was the only good part of the afternoon.

Auntie Kim swooped into the kitchen and gave Mattie a big hug. 'How wonderful! You've come at just the right time.'

She took Mattie and rushed her into the hall, to a large cupboard which was stuffed with costumes. 'Now,' she said, ruffling through the cupboard, 'here's a lovely dandelion costume.'

Mattie's heart sank into her gym shoes. A dandelion! Oh no!

'Isn't this bee-yewtiful?' sighed Auntie Kim. 'Lucky you and Sharon are just the same size.'

Before she had time to protest, Mattie was whisked out of her clothes and thrust into bright green tights, a ghastly dress with yellow stripes and stuck-on green bits, and a stupid head-dress with sprouting yellow fronds coming out of the top of it. The children gathered round to stare at her, and Mattie stuck out her tongue.

'Now, now,' cried Auntie Kim. 'That's no way for a Gem to behave. You are now representing Madame Wanda, and I have my reputation to uphold.'

Mattie stood with her legs apart and her arms folded across her chest.

'Child!' squeaked Auntie Kim, 'You are a dandelion, not a rugby player. Stand nicely.'

Mattie tried to 'stand nicely'. She slumped her shoulders and put her hands on her hips.

'Hm,' said Auntie Kim. 'I can see I'm going to have my work cut out with *you*. I'll go through the songs and dances with you later. Not all my Gems get extra tuition you know. I hope you're grateful.'

Mattie thought she could get extra tuition till she was blue in the face, but she wouldn't be grateful. Then Auntie Kim gave her some song-sheets and told her to go and learn the words. Mattie did not like the words of any of these songs. She did not want to sing them. In fact she did not want to have anything to do with the Little Gems.

The only thing to do was to run away, Mattie

decided. There were two problems: one, she was dressed as a dandelion and two, she had no money for the bus. So she put her thinking cap on. That was what her mother always said when there was a problem: 'I'll have to put my thinking cap on.' Mattie knew it wasn't a real cap, but she imagined the cap all the same. It was red wool with a little silk tassel.

Feeling rather desperate, Mattie looked round the kitchen. There was a little pile of money on the breakfast bar. She found a pencil and tore the corner off a paper bag in the bread-bin. She wrote 'I.O.U. twenty pence,' and she took two ten-pence pieces and left the note instead. She knew that was what you should do when you borrowed money.

She decided bravely that she would just have to bear the ride home on the bus, with everyone

laughing at her dandelion costume and calling out remarks the way people did. Just because you happened to be wearing a silly costume, people always thought they could say what they liked and it wouldn't hurt or make you feel hot and miserable.

Mattie went quietly out of the kitchen and down the fire escape to the street. At the bus stop three people were waiting: a man, an old lady and a boy. Mattie tried to look as though she happened to be dressed up as a dandelion only because she felt like it.

The boy put his hand up to his mouth and Mattie knew he was laughing at her. She fixed him with a very stony look but he went on giggling.

The man folded up the paper he had been reading and said, 'Well, well, well, young lady. Have you escaped from the circus?'

Mattie did not think that was at all funny, so she turned her back on him and the old lady said, 'Dear me. No manners either. It's disgusting.'

Then the 45 bus came along and Mattie hoped it wouldn't be full.

The bus conductor smiled and said, 'Spring has sprung. It's Miss Buttercup herself!'

'Dandelion actually,' muttered Mattie. If people were going to be rude to her, they might at least be correct.

'Oh-oh. Little Miss Dandelion. I do beg your pardon,' he said, bowing to her as she sat down. Everyone stared.

Mattie nearly cried. She was so upset that she almost missed her stop and she had to run down the bus and jump off just as the bus was starting off again.

'Mind how you go, little Miss Dandelion,' called the driver, and the passengers waved and banged on the windows.

Mattie decided that when she was grown up, even if a child got on a bus dressed as a giant fir tree, she would not say a word about it. There could be any number of reasons why a child might be dressed as a giant fir tree, decided Mattie as she stamped up the road to her house.

She rang the doorbell and her mother rushed to the door, grabbed her by her yellow fronds and pulled her into the hall. 'Where have you *been*?'

yelled her mother. 'Auntie Kim was just about to ring the police. You naughty girl!' And she shook Mattie. 'Auntie Kim was in floods of tears. We thought you'd been kidnapped. I *knew* this would happen!'

Mattie took off her hat and said, 'I did the only sensible thing. I hate Auntie Kim. I hate Samantha. I hate Madame Wanda and all her Little Gems. And most of all I hate this silly dress and stupid hat. So now you know.'

Mattie followed her mother into the sitting room.

'But you wanted to go,' said Mrs McCrum in a tired voice. 'I told you that you might not like it. You knew what they were like.'

Mattie felt sad and fed up. 'Well I thought I would like it once I got there,' she said. 'I didn't know I was going to be made into a Little Gem, did I?'

'I suppose not,' said Mrs McCrum, 'but you've caused an awful lot of bother. I'll have to ring Auntie Kim and explain, and I don't know what I'm going to say.'

'You can say I've always been a strange child,' said Mattie. 'Then she'll feel sorry for you.'

'I expect she does anyway,' said her mother.

Mattie went upstairs to her bedroom. She lay on the bed and closed her eyes. She felt tired and her head ached.

Next weekend she was going to stay with Jolly Uncle Jack. *If* they let her.

'Well at least I didn't have to be a Little Gem,' thought Mattie. Then just before she fell asleep she heard her mother saying to Auntie Kim:

'You see dear, I'm afraid she's always been a very *strange* child.'

3

Jolly Uncle Jack

Mattie woke up on Saturday morning and remembered that this weekend was going to be spent with jolly Uncle Jack.

Her heart sank. But as she had pestered and nagged and 'driven her mother round the bend', until she had been allowed to go, Mattie now had no choice.

'Uncle Jack's not mad really,' Mattie told herself before she got out of bed. 'If I try very hard I'm sure I can have a nice time.'

She tried hard to think of all the good things about Uncle Jack. She managed to make a short list:

1 He's got a huge collection of toys.
2 There's never any long, awkward silences when I'm with him.
3 He's always got time to play.

Hmm. She thought of her grandmother's favourite saying: 'You've made your bed and now you must lie on it.'

Mattie knew this meant that if a thing was your own fault you couldn't complain about it.

It made Mattie laugh because if there was one thing Mattie never did it was make her bed. It always seemed too much trouble. Mattie would just hump the covers over her head and wriggle down in the crumpled sheets. Then she would feel cross and uncomfortable all night. But she was still too lazy to make her bed.

Mattie began to pack her small suitcase. She knew she didn't have to take any games because Uncle Jack's house was like a toy shop.

He had jigsaws, Scrabble, Monopoly, Cluedo, Ludo, Hospital, Scoop, Careers, Flying Hats, Chinese Chequers, darts, draughts, chess, backgammon, quizzes and a funny Chinese game called Mah Jong with lots of little coloured bricks or 'tiles' as Uncle Jack said they had to be called.

He also had bows and arrows, fishing rods, pea shooters, Red Indian head-dresses, cowboy outfits, cricket bats, footballs, skipping ropes, sailing boats and a doll's house.

Uncle Jack thought that every moment should be filled with activity.

'I shall need a hearty breakfast,' Mattie told her mother as she went into the kitchen. 'You know how hard Jolly Uncle Jack makes me work. Last time, as soon as I stopped playing tiddlywinks we had to play Flying Hats and when that was over nine people came round and we played a stupid game called Sardines for about two hours. I was worn out!'

Mrs McCrum looked at her. 'Are you complaining?' she said.

'Of course not,' Mattie replied as she spooned up her two boiled eggs. 'I was only *saying*.'

After she had eaten the eggs she had a mug of cocoa, two slices of toast and honey, and half an apple.

'I'll need something for the journey,' she told her mother. 'I don't suppose we'll have time to eat once I'm there.'

Mrs McCrum sighed. She made up a parcel of ham sandwiches and currant cake.

'I ought to have some crisps too,' said Mattie. 'Just in case.'

When Mattie arrived at Uncle Jack's, he came to the door with a table tennis bat in his hand, wearing a tall chef's hat which said BORN TO BAKE on it.

'Mattie,' he boomed in his loud voice. 'Do come in my dear child. You're just in time for a game.'

'I'd better unpack first,' said Mattie hopefully.

'Nonsense. Nonsense,' he said 'I know you can't wait to try out my new table-tennis game. It's wonderful.' He hustled Mattie into one of his large rooms and gave her a bat.

'I'll serve,' he cried and whacked the ball at Mattie.

'Oh dear,' thought Mattie as she missed the ball. 'I could be at home reading or arranging my china cats.'

The ball rolled under the sideboard and she had

to scrabble about until she found it.

'When we've finished this game,' said Uncle Jack, 'I'm going to make some biscuits for tea and then we'll have a nice game of cricket before we go out. I'm in a new show with The Arcadian Players in town. I've got a ticket for you. Won't that be lovely?'

Mattie felt like falling asleep at the thought of all this activity ahead. 'Yes . . . . lovely,' she said in a small voice.

After a very hectic game of cricket during which Mattie scored no runs and didn't manage to catch the ball once, they went in for tea.

During the meal they had to have a quiz, of course. Mattie tried hard to answer questions on the world's longest river, the highest mountain, the largest lake and the smallest animal.

'Knowledge should be FUN,' said Uncle Jack but Mattie didn't say anything because she wanted to go and change for the theatre and she hoped that if she didn't encourage him Uncle Jack wouldn't ask her anything else.

'Watch out for me at the theatre,' he said 'I play three parts – a waiter, a villain and a Duke!'

Mattie wondered if he was going to play them all at the same time. You never knew with Jolly Uncle Jack!

At the theatre Mattie was given a seat in the middle of the front row. She wished she had been able to sit in the balcony because she could see some boys dropping lollipop sticks onto people's heads below and it looked fun.

She sat next to a friend of Uncle Jack's called Mrs Overpond. She was large with grey curls and a coat with a big fur collar. She kept eating chocolates but she only offered Mattie one, which Mattie thought was rather mean.

The curtain went up and there was Uncle Jack dressed as a villain with a false moustache and a swirling satin cape. Mattie kept thinking about the BORN TO BAKE hat and she smiled.

'Don't smile,' said Mrs Overpond in a shocked whisper. 'This is TRAGIC.'

Mattie could not see that it was tragic at all. In fact, she thought it was funny because the scenery kept wobbling and Uncle Jack's moustache looked as though it was coming unstuck.

Someone was seen in the wings sticking out their tongue and when a shot was fired it went off a few seconds too late because the actress had already fallen down. This was too much for Mattie – she had to force a handkerchief into her mouth to quell a fit of giggles.

Mrs Overpond kept dabbing her eyes and muttering 'Oh too tragic . . . too tragic.' Then the play was over and Mattie felt pleased. Mrs Overpond ate two more chocolates and clapped loudly calling 'Encore . . . encore' as Uncle Jack took his bow.

Just as Mattie was putting on her coat Uncle Jack came to the front of the stage. 'As you know,' he said, 'after the show we like to have a little talent contest. Anybody who wants to come up and sing a song or recite will be very welcome.'

Everyone clapped and then Uncle Jack said something which made Mattie feel sick and go cold all over.

'I can see a little girl on the front row in a red dress,' he said, 'and I think she'd like to come up here with me and sing to you all.'

'Oh YES,' roared the crowd.

'Oh NO!' roared Mattie, and before anyone could stop her she leapt up and ran to the back of the theatre where the ice-cream lady was.

'Hide me . . . quick!' begged Mattie. The lady

opened a door marked PRIVATE and Mattie ran inside.

The room had a warm biscuity smell and seemed to be full of cartons labelled 'Popcorn', 'Peanuts' and 'Orange Juice'.

Just reading the names made Mattie feel hungry. She wondered if Uncle Jack would run after her and drag her up on stage – surely he wouldn't be that cruel.

Mattie could hear everyone laughing. How DARE they? THIS was even worse than her day with Auntie Kim. If THEY think it's funny let THEM get up and sing. Then Uncle Jack said, 'Ho ... ho ... she's run off like a little rabbit.'

Mattie opened the door just enough to peep out. To her relief she saw a girl skip up onto the stage wearing a pink, flounced dress. She stood there smiling and did a few dainty dance steps.

'Aaaaaah,' said the crowd.

'Well now,' said Uncle Jack.

'Ugh!' said Mattie.

'How nice,' said Uncle Jack, beaming. 'This young lady is going to dance for us.'

Mattie leant against the door. 'Phew,' she said. 'Thank goodness. At least they'll leave me alone now.'

She wondered how she was going to get to Uncle Jack's dressing room without him noticing.

She knew she couldn't go home in the dark by herself. Then she noticed a rack of costumes: a cat outfit, two sailor suits and lots of evening dresses with velvet capes.

Someone had been dressed as a cat in the show so Mattie decided to wear the cat costume and pretend she'd been one of the players if anyone spoke to her. Then she could creep round to Uncle Jack's dressing room and wait for him.

She quickly put the outfit on. It was very hot and rather big but Mattie didn't care. She straightened the tail and unfolded the ears, then opened the door a crack.

The ice-cream lady had gone. The girl in the pink dress was singing 'Underneath The Arches' and the audience as still saying 'Aaaaaah' as Mattie crept out and to the STAGE DOOR AND EXIT sign. She bounded down the corridor but a young man was coming towards her.

'Hallo Peggy,' he said. 'Super performance tonight. Want to go for dinner?'

Mattie shook her head. 'Dousy cowd,' she said in a hoarse whisper and ran off.

'A COLD?' said the astonished young man.

But Mattie had disappeared into the dressing room. No one was there so she took off the cat costume, which was making her very hot, and sat down.

Quite soon Uncle Jack came in. 'Goodness me, Mattie!' he exclaimed. 'I've been looking for you everywhere.'

Mattie gave him an apologetic smile. 'I'm sorry,' she said, 'but performing is my least favourite thing in all the world.'

'Oh dear me,' he said. 'What a FUNNY little article you are!' Then he laughed.

'Well nobody else seems to want to perform to-night so we'll go home. But first I must find poor Peggy. I hear she's got a terrible cold and is feeling very ill. I had no idea.'

The door opened and a healthy-looking girl with rosy cheeks popped in.

'Hallo Jack,' she said. 'I just came to say good-bye. I'm off now.'

'Hallo Peggy,' said Uncle Jack, 'I thought you were ill.'

'Me?' said Peggy, astounded. 'Ill? No. Don't know where you got that from. I'm as fit as a fiddle.'

Then she went and Mattie had a quick conversation with herself:

'IF you tell them it was you in the cat costume it'll cause a big fuss.

'THEN they'll all laugh at you and call you a funny little article.

'THEN they might be cross so it isn't worth it. After all, you didn't do anything WRONG.'

So she sat very still and didn't say a word.

'That's very strange ... about Peggy,' said Uncle Jack. 'Must've been a mix-up. Oh well.'

When they got home Uncle Jack made a jug of cocoa and they had two games of 'Snap', then 'I Spy' and after that Mattie had to guess the number of lentils in a jar. She went up to bed feeling quite worn out.

Uncle Jack called up the stairs, 'What year was Queen Elizabeth the Second crowned?'

But Mattie didn't answer. She pretended to be fast alseep.

4

The biggest fusspot in the world

Mrs McCrum looked at Mattie with what Mattie called her weary expression, as though everything was too much for her, especially Mattie.

Mr McCrum said, 'I'm not going to argue about this . . . it's all very silly.'

He went into the garden. Although he didn't like gardening at all he liked walking round the lawn deciding what needed doing and where he was going to plant things. He spent many happy hours *planning* the perfect garden which nobody would ever see.

Mattie folded her arms across her chest which was her habit when she was annoyed.

'And don't look like that,' said Mrs McCrum. 'You ran away from Auntie Kim's . . . you were so tired when you came back from Uncle Jack's that you had to have a morning in bed . . . PLUS there was a lot of nonsense about you impersonating a cat. I just don't think it's worth it.'

'But I CAN'T get into trouble at Aunt Marion's,' said Mattie. 'She's so clean and quiet it's as though nobody lives there at all.'

'Yes,' said Mrs McCrum 'And that's what worries me. You know how fussy she is.'

'Oh Mum. I'd be very neat and good. It might be just the thing ... I mean I'd HAVE to be neat and good while I was there and it might sort of stay with me when I got back.'

'I suppose miracles do happen,' said her mother doubtfully. She sighed. 'All right then ... I suppose you can go. But you MUST behave yourself.'

'Oh I WILL,' promised Mattie but Mrs McCrum did not look convinced.

Mr McCrum groaned when he heard the news, then he clutched his head and looked at the sky. He spent a long time in the garden, and by tea time he had landscaped the front and back gardens and built a white summer house and two fish ponds, all in his imagination.

Aunt Marion lived in a house so small it was almost like a doll's house. Aunt Marion was not unlike a doll herself. She had a neat face and blue eyes and curls that never seemed to move, even on the windiest day.

Her clothes never needed mending or looked creased or had crumbs or doghairs on them, even though she had a dog. He was a Yorkshire Terrier called Truffle and he wore bows to match Aunt Marion's clothes.

Her kitchen sparkled and there was a sign on the wall saying:

A PLACE FOR EVERYTHING
AND EVERYTHING IN ITS PLACE.

Mattie had plaited her hair to look tidy but she had done it so tightly that her face was stretched back, giving her a rather startled look!

When she arrived she put her case down in the hall. 'No ... no ...' squeaked Aunt Marion. 'I've just been over that floor with a soft cloth and bees-wax ... you'll mark it.'

Mattie picked the case up again.

'Take it upstairs to the front bedroom. Then you can wash your face and hands and we'll have a cup of tea.'

The bedroom was not at all like Mattie's. Hers was full of headless dolls, old teddybears, spilt games, biscuits and half-finished paintings. This one was like a room in an advertisement ... or one of those little pretend rooms in department stores. It smelt of lavender. The brass bell by the bed had a little lace cloth on it; the tissue holder wore a satin crinoline lady; the comb on the dressing table was in a plastic case and even the cushion on the chair had a cellophane wrapper.

'She'll probably put a cover over me,' thought Mattie, imagining Aunt Marion popping a green cloth over her as though she were a parrot in a cage.

Mattie washed her hands twice and hung the towel up neatly instead of flinging it on the floor as she usually did. Then she went downstairs without sliding down the banisters or jumping the stairs two at a time with a handstand to finish, which was her favourite way.

When she went into the dining room she felt she ought to curtsy. In fact, she gave a polite little bob just for her own amusement but Aunt Marion didn't seem to notice.

The polished table was laid for tea. The china cups had pink bows on them and on the cake-stand were the thinnest slices of cake and the smallest walnut buns that Mattie had ever seen.

'Sit right up to the table,' said Aunt Marion. 'Then you won't make crumbs on the carpet.'

Mattie wondered whether Aunt Marion would tell her to swallow everything whole so she wouldn't make crumbs in her mouth!

Mattie took two wafer-thin slices of bread, a little triangle of cake and a walnut bun.

'Goodness child,' exclaimed Aunt Marion, 'You'll POP.'

Mattie ate them very quickly because she was hungry. She was just reaching for another bun when Aunt Marion gave her a warning glance.

'Don't you think you've had enough, my dear? We don't want you to have stomach-ache.'

Mattie felt like saying that the only time she got stomach-ache was when she was hungry, but she didn't.

Then Aunt Marion went out to fill the teapot again. Truffle was in his basket near the fire.

Rapidly, Mattie ate four cakes, three biscuits and some more bread and then she flung some crumbs into the dog's basket.

Aunt Marion came back. She stared at the cake stand in amazement.

'Oh dear,' said Mattie sounding worried. 'I'm afraid Truffle just . . . jumped up onto the table and before I could stop him, he'd eaten lots and lots.'

Instead of being cross, as Mattie expected, Aunt Marion rushed over to his basket and fussed over Truffle.

'Oh darling diddum-widdums,' she said. 'And WAS he hungry and DID Mummy not give him enough? Naughty Mummy ... oh ... poor, poor Truffle.' She scooped him up and walked about stroking him but Mattie thought Truffle didn't look very happy. She felt glad that she hadn't got him into trouble but it didn't seem fair of Aunt Marion to behave as though Truffle was starving to death. He was quite a fat little dog.

'I'm the one who's still hungry,' thought Mattie.

Aunt Marion put Truffle back in his basket and said she would find some chicken for him. Then she turned to Mattie.

'As a treat this afternoon I thought you could run an errand for me,' she said. 'I've made some linen tray cloths for the Ladies' Circle Bring-and-Buy. If you could take them to Saint Peter's church for me I'd be very grateful.'

Mattie decided that even this would be better than trying not to make crumbs all day.

'When you come back you can help me wind some wool.'

Mattie tried not to look ill with boredom.

'You'd better have a wash before you go out,' said Aunt Marion.

'I've only just HAD a wash,' complained Mattie but she went upstairs. Instead of going into

the bathroom, she played with the roller-blind in her room, seeing how quickly she could get it to unroll. Unfortunately it rolled itself back so fast that it was too tightly wound to come down again.

'Oops,' said Mattie, as she turned and ran down the stairs. She only just remembered to stop in time to enter the room in her best ladylike manner.

She set off with the tray cloths 'beautifully folded in fresh tissue paper', and looked in the shops on the way. She walked past the toy shop and the sweet shop but she went into the newsagents. She began to read the new comics hoping the assistant wouldn't notice – but she did!

'Oi! You!' she yelled, 'Are you going to buy those?'

Mattie ran out of the shop and up the road until she saw a church with a notice outside:

SAINT PAUL'S CHURCH
JUMBLE SALE TODAY 2PM.

'This must be it,' thought Mattie. 'A jumble sale is the same as a Bring-and-Buy.'

She went into a hut in the churchyard which was full of people pushing and shoving and saying things like, 'Keep STILL Tracey while I see if this fits you.'

Mattie found a table with cloths and tea towels on it and handed her parcel to the lady in charge.

'These are tray cloths from Miss McCrum,' said Mattie.

The lady unwrapped them.

'Ooh, these ARE nice,' she said. 'Thank you

love. They'll go very well.'

She stuck a ticket on them which said seventy-five pence each and put them on the table.

Mattie went out wondering where she could go so she wouldn't have to go back and wind wool. As she went along a different route she saw another church. The large notice outside said:

SAINT PETER'S CHURCH
LADIES' CIRCLE BRING-AND-BUY

'Oh NO!' Mattie suddenly realised what she had done! She rushed back to Saint Paul's but the tray cloths had gone.

'Snapped up love,' said the woman. 'Gone in a moment. As soon as I put them down.'

Mattie didn't know what to do. Then she saw four very old, worn tray cloths marked at five pence each.

'I'll have those please,' she said quickly.

The woman thought Mattie was very strange but Mattie found twenty pence after hunting in all her pockets and she ran out and into Saint Peter's Bring-and-Buy Sale.

It was very quiet. Two elderly ladies were arranging the stalls very carefully. One was for home-made jam and cakes and another had lovely embroidery and tapestry on it.

'These are the tray cloths from Miss McCrum,' gabbled Mattie.

'Oh thank you, my dear,' said one. 'She does such wonderful work ... it's always such a joy to look at.'

She examined the cloths Mattie held out. Her face fell and she said, 'Er ... is ... has Miss McCrum been ill lately?'

'Oh no. She's very well indeed,' said Mattie as she hurried out of the church. 'I'm sure they won't find out,' she told herself, trying not to worry. 'After all, how could they? No one knows.'

When she got back she had to wipe her feet and brush her hair, then Aunt Marion said, 'What did they say to you about my tray cloths? Were they pleased with them?'

'Oh YES,' cried Mattie. 'They said your work was wonderful and a joy to look at.'

'Well, that's very strange,' said Aunt Marion in a cross, puzzled voice.

'Oh, why?' asked Mattie sweetly.

'Because I had a telephone call from Saint Peter's church saying they were disappointed with the standard of work I had sent and they didn't know whether they would be able to display it or not. That's why!

'I've never been more insulted in my life. I said to Mrs Fellows ... if that's the way you feel about my tray cloths you can get somebody else to do them next year. I banged the telephone down and

37

I've never done that in my life!'

'Oh dear,' said Mattie. 'Perhaps they're being extra fussy this year. They did have a lot of VERY nice tapestry.'

'Oh did they indeed?' said Aunt Marion. 'Well, they can keep it!'

Mattie sighed. She wondered why she was always having to keep quiet about things that happened to her when none of them was really her fault. Aunt Marion was in a sour mood for the rest of the day and kept saying, 'Tapestry. HUMPH!' in a disgusted tone.

Mattie was glad when bedtime came, even though she couldn't get the blind down and had to tell Aunt Marion that she ALWAYS slept with the blind up at home!

All Aunt Marion said was, 'Tapestry indeed!'

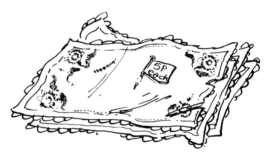

5

Stanley and the wedding

'Mattie, for the tenth time will you PLEASE stand still,' begged Mrs McCrum. Or rather she said, 'Mappy, wiw you pleafe ftand ftill,' because she had a mouthful of pins. She was finishing a dress for Mattie. It was a bridesmaid's dress and Mrs McCrum was taking up the hem and trying to make Mattie look 'as pretty as a picture'.

That was what cousin Laura had said when she asked for Mattie to be bridesmaid at her wedding, 'I want her to look dainty and as pretty as a picture.'

Mrs McCrum did not say that dainty and pretty as a picture were two things she had never known Mattie look ... but then that did rather depend on which picture was meant! She just smiled and said Mattie would be delighted to walk down the aisle with a basket of rose petals and a silver horseshoe. Mattie, however, was not at all delighted.

'Me?' she squawked when she heard the news. 'You must be joking. Got up like a dog's dinner and scattering flower petals. You must be joking!'

Mrs McCrum said that she couldn't let the family down and it was all arranged.

'Well,' said Mattie crossly. 'When I'm grown up I'm not going to make arrangements for people without asking them first. It's very rude. AND unfair.'

It was even worse when she found out that Laura had chosen the dress material, the shoes AND the head-dress for her.

Mattie stared at them all in disgust. 'Have I got to wear that on my head? It looks like bird sick.'

'Don't be silly, Mattie,' said her mother in a warning voice. 'It's very expensive white chiffon and lace with a coronet of seed pearls.'

'Hah!' said Mattie. 'Well, seeing as the dress is going to reach the floor, couldn't I wear my baseball boots instead of those satin things? No one would see.'

'No you cannot,' shouted Mrs McCrum. 'Oh I do wish you hadn't been asked. Life would be so much easier.'

She held up the pink material for the dress and Mattie made horrible noises.

'I'll look like a marzipan pig in that,' she said. 'All pink and shiny.'

'Oh be quiet,' said her mother, flicking Mattie with the end of her tape measure.

'If Laura wants a pig walking down the aisle behind her she's MAD, that's all I can say.'

'Mattie. If I hear one more word of complaint out of you I'll make this dress so tight you won't be able to breathe and you'll pop out of it in church.'

'Oh good,' said Mattie. 'That'd be fun.'

The wedding was on Saturday. On Friday evening the dress was still not ready and that was why Mrs McCrum was holding pins in her mouth and saying 'ftand ftill' to Mattie.

'I've never stood still so much in my whole life. If I stand any more still I'll turn to stone.'

'Now . . .' said Mrs McCrum. 'Let's just pop the head-dress on and see how it all looks.'

Mattie scowled and ducked her head so the coronet of seed pearls slid over one eye. Mrs McCrum laughed.

'You do look a wonderful sight. Perhaps cousin Laura will have second thoughts when she sees you.'

'I wish she'd have them now,' said Mattie darkly.

When the dress was ready, Mattie hoped she would be allowed to run off and play. No such luck!

'I want you to have an early night so you don't look tired tomorrow and I want you to wash your hair nicely.'

Mattie went into the bathroom. First of all she squirted her father's shaving foam over the mirror. She did a picture of a small pig in the bridesmaid's dress. Then she made some soap gloves for herself when she washed her hands. She decided to have long evening gloves that reached up to her elbows.

When she'd done that she didn't know how to get rid of the soap which was frothing and billowing about so she wiped it off on both the clean towels.

She found a bottle of her mother's nail varnish and painted her toe-nails Hot Pink. She wasn't very neat so some of her toes were Hot Pink too. Then she thought it would be fun to try out a new and wonderful hairstyle for the wedding.

First of all she pinned up her hair. Then she went into Mrs McCrum's bedroom and borrowed some ribbon, feathers, two pencils, a long piece of lace, a bit of curtain wire and a large silk rose.

She arranged all these things in her hair and sprayed it to make it set. She was just admiring the effect when her mother called up the stairs.

'When you've dried your hair get into bed and I'll bring you some cocoa.'

'Oh help,' thought Mattie.

She started to make a low-pitched buzzing noise hoping to sound like the hair dryer but all her mother said was, 'Stop making that silly noise and get into bed.'

Mattie quickly pulled all the bits and pieces out of her hair and threw some water on it to look as though she had washed it. Then she flung off her clothes and jumped into bed in her underwear. She pulled the covers up to her neck and sat waiting for her cocoa.

'That's a good girl,' said Mrs McCrum as she came in with the tray. 'Your hair still looks a bit damp though.'

'Oh no . . . it's fine,' said Mattie, gulping down her cocoa and hoping her mother wouldn't look in the bathroom. Luckily Mrs McCrum had a lot to do that evening so she soon went downstairs to help Mr McCrum press his best trousers for the wedding and to sew a ribbon round her straw hat.

Mr McCrum was not in a good mood. He found weddings rather boring.

'They're all the same,' he said. 'Same words, same music, same food, same drink, same dress, same people half the time.'

'Oh don't be so silly . . . you'll enjoy it when you get there. You know what you're like. I don't know

... you and Mattie are such a pair. Nothing's ever right for you!'

'If I never see another sausage on a cocktail stick again, it'll be too soon,' continued Mr McCrum, ironing his trousers and not taking any notice of Mrs McCrum who was full of sighs and head shakings.

The wedding morning did not begin well.

Just before breakfast it was discovered that Mattie had taken Stanley the cat up to bed with her to keep her company. Stanley liked sleeping in or on hats and when he found Mattie's bridesmaid's head-dress in the middle of the night, he curled himself up on it for a nice long sleep. Stanley was not a slender cat. He was round and hefty and his fat paws were covered in thick fur which made him look even bigger.

Mrs McCrum flew into a rage while Mattie hotly defended him.

'It's not HIS fault. He's a CAT. He can't tell a head-dress from an ordinary hat – even though he is very intelligent,' she added hastily in case Stanley heard her.

'Look at this. Just LOOK at it. All bent and filthy.'

'Stanley isn't filthy. He loves washing himself. Apart from eating, it's his favourite thing.'

'MUST we stand here discussing the cat's personal habits?' said Mr McCrum. He had been ready for an hour and was feeling irritable. He would much rather be planning a garden or watching a cricket match with his friends than going to the wedding.

Mattie was sent upstairs to get dressed while Mrs McCrum tried to press the head-dress back into shape. 'I just hope Laura will be too busy to notice,' she said.

Stanley knew that he was in trouble, and he was lying in the middle of Mattie's bed looking hunted and miserable. Mattie gathered him up.

'Oh poor Stanley. It's not your fault. I wish you could come to church with me. Wouldn't you like to scatter rose petals and have lots of silly old relatives kissing you and saying "Oh . . . hasn't she grown? Last time I saw her she was only THIS high." And everyone addresses remarks about you to your mother as though you don't exist and you haven't got a tongue. "And how is Mattie doing at school?" And, "Is she over her bad cold?" And, "Should she be eating all that cake?" You're very lucky really, Stanley.'

Stanley closed his eyes and purred. He put his big furry paws round Mattie's neck and hugged him.

Mrs McCrum came in looking very rushed and hot. When she saw Mattie and Stanley she was very cross.

'Please put that cat down and get ready. You

can't walk down the aisle with cat hairs all over you.'

Mattie put Stanley on the bed and got into her bridesmaid's dress. She pulled a face when she looked in the mirror.

'What do you think Stanley? Aren't you ashamed of me . . . all dressed up like a pink pig? I don't blame you,' she said as she saw that Stanley had turned his head away and closed his eyes.

Mattie was supposed to wear lace socks with little pink rosebuds sewn on the side. She hated them. They were scratchy and her toes kept poking through the holes in the lace which made them feel as if they were being cut off. She decided to wear her favourite socks instead. They were red and yellow striped wool and they were quite old so they felt soft and comfortable. 'No one will notice. They'll be too busy looking at Laura.'

She put her old socks on. Unfortunately the dress didn't quite cover her feet, and yellow and red are not the ideal colours to wear with pale pink, but Mattie didn't care.

Mr McCrum was already tooting the horn outside and Mrs McCrum shouted up the stairs, 'I'm taking your head-dress with me. Now come and get in the car at once!'

Mattie ran her fingers through her hair, rubbed at an ink stain on her elbow and then she was ready.

'Oh Stanley ... I think you should come with me,' she decided suddenly. She picked him up and ran downstairs with him, as Mrs McCrum was getting into the car. Mattie popped the cat into a large canvas shopping bag and put two comics and a rainhat on top of him.

'Be a good, quiet boy, Stanley ... please,'

begged Mattie, and Stanley obligingly snuggled down in the bag and began to snooze.

'What on earth have you got in there?' asked her mother.

'Oh just some comfortable shoes for the journey home and a few comics to read,' said Mattie.

'Well sit very carefully and don't squash anything, and mind Laura's present . . . it's a tea set.'

'She's probably got about ninety tea sets already,' said Mattie. 'I shouldn't think she'd want another one. I mean, if I was getting married I wouldn't want more than one tea set . . . nobody normal would want ninety tea sets, I shouldn't think.'

Mrs McCrum threw a barley sugar at Mattie to shut her up. It hit her on the nose.

'I somehow get the impression you want me to be quiet,' said Mattie. The McCrum family continued their journey in silence.

When they got to the church a great crowd of friends and relatives swooped on them. 'Like a big flock of vultures,' whispered Mattie to Stanley. 'Here we go.'

'And HOW is little Mattie?' asked Great Aunt Rose, looking at Mrs McCrum.

'Little Mattie's fine thank you,' said Mattie.

Great Aunt Rose looked very surprised.

'How's Great Aunt Rose?' Mattie asked Uncle Wilfred. He looked confused.

'Er ... well ... as you can see ... she's fine.'

'Oh THAT'S nice,' said Mattie, smiling at Uncle Wilfred. 'And is her cold better?'

'Oh yes,' he said.

'Is the child not capable of speaking to me herself?' asked Great Aunt Rose, which made Mattie laugh.

Mrs McCrum had to take Mattie into the cloakroom at the church and adjust her head-dress and smooth her frock.

'You do look a bit crumpled,' she said worriedly.

'And why on earth did you carry on in that silly way with Aunt Rose?'

'Because Aunt Rose carried on in a silly way with me,' said Mattie.

'Oh, I haven't time for your nonsense now,' Mrs McCrum said. 'I'm going to sit in the church. Don't forget ... you wait in the porch until Laura arrives.'

As soon as her mother had gone Mattie took Stanley out of the bag and tied a ribbon onto his collar.

'You must be very good,' she told him. 'The goodest you've ever been in your whole life.' Stanley narrowed his eyes. Then he yawned. 'Look happy, Stanley. It's a wedding,' she told him.

The church was packed with people and Mattie ran with Stanley round the back of the church and into the porch. She was just in time because Laura drove up in a white car with satin ribbons on the bonnet, and a man in a peaked cap at the wheel.

'Coo,' said Mattie.

Laura stepped out looking cross. 'My tights have just laddered,' she told Mattie. 'So don't hold my train up too high in case people notice my ankles.'

'I know what you mean,' said Mattie. Luckily everyone seemed so busy with their own problems that they hadn't noticed Mattie's striped socks. Laura didn't even see Stanley. He was lurking behind Mattie and arched his back when the organ began playing *Here Comes The Bride*.

Laura's father took her arm and they all began to walk down the aisle. Mattie held the train very carefully and Stanley trotted obediently behind them, his ribbon still in place.

Mrs McCrum was just thinking what a charming picture her darling little Mattie made and that she DID know how to behave properly after all. She glanced down and suddenly said 'Oh NO!' out loud. Everyone turned round. She had noticed the socks!

'Look. LOOK!' she hissed to Mr McCrum, who was miles away drinking cold beer in the cricket pavilion and being congratulated on his spectacular score.

'Oh . . . Oh! She's brought the CAT!'

'Sssh,' said the people in front.

'Do something!' moaned Mrs McCrum.

'Oh . . . the child's SOCKS!' exclaimed Great Aunt Rose.

'Look . . . there's a cat,' said Wilfred.

'I knew we shouldn't have come,' sighed Mr McCrum.

Mattie couldn't hear any of this. She scattered rose petals and smiled at Stanley and, like the good and intelligent cat he was, he sat beside Mattie as the vicar began to speak.

Everyone in the church had noticed the socks and Stanley by now. There was whispering and shuffling and craning of necks. People said 'Fancy!' and 'Dear me!' and 'I think it's terrible'. Poor Mrs McCrum felt like running away.

The vicar seemed to be droning on for a long time. Suddenly Stanley gave a big yawn and this made people giggle. They kept trying to disguise their giggles as coughs and sneezes but the vicar looked very cross.

'Wait until I get hold of her,' muttered Mrs McCrum.

'Please . . . sssh,' said Mr McCrum. 'I'm just going in to bat . . . don't distract me.'

Mrs McCrum decided that not only did she have an uncontrollable daughter, she had got a

mad husband too!

When the ceremony was over, the bridal procession began its walk up the aisle. Mattie tried not to look at her mother, but she could feel Mrs McCrum's eyes boring into her so she gave a quick look, the way you would if you knew there was something frightening across the room but you couldn't resist having a peep. Great Aunt Rose lifted her eyebrows at her and Uncle Wilfred shook his head. The only person who didn't admonish her with a strange expression was her father. He had just scored eighty runs so all was well in his world.

'What a circus,' said Laura.

Just then Stanley saw a mouse. Stanley couldn't resist mice. He growled and sprang forward right between Laura's ankles. She fell over and lay sprawled in the aisle as everyone pushed forward to help.

One of the cousins with a camera ran forward and took a photograph of Laura. She burst into tears when she realised what he had done and scrambled to her feet shouting at him.

The mouse ran under a pew and Stanley dived between Great Aunt Rose's ankles and clawed at her new brown suede shoes thinking they might be mice.

Wilfred swatted Stanley with his hymn book but he missed and hit Rose on the knee instead. She gave a yelp of pain and jumped up.

Mattie knelt down and scuttled along past Rose and Wilfred, trying to grab hold of Stanley who had spotted a lovely straw hat on somebody's lap and decided it was just the thing to curl up on and go to sleep.

Mattie caught him just in time. Everybody clustered round her.

Laura was crying. Wilfred was laughing. Mrs McCrum said she was 'beyond words' and Mr McCrum kept trying to look cross but Mattie knew him too well and realised that he was trying not to smile.

Mr McCrum decided that Mattie should be punished and said that he would have to take her home. 'Although it breaks my heart to leave this happy gathering,' he said, looking sad.

Laura generously said that Mattie would be sent some cake and kissed her goodbye. Great Aunt Rose said Mattie didn't deserve cake and Wilfred gave her a hug and whispered, 'Best wedding I've been to.'

'You weren't really heart-broken, were you?' Mattie asked her father as they drove home.

'No,' he said, smiling. 'Of course I wasn't. The champagne would have been nice but at least now I can watch the cricket this afternoon. Shall we buy some fish and chips?'

Mattie felt very pleased. She knew all the relatives would complain about her but after all, she HAD done her duty as bridesmaid and Laura DID get married and Stanley had an exciting day out.

'It was good fun wasn't it Stanley?' she asked him.

But Stanley was in a deep sleep on the back seat, right on top of Mattie's head-dress.

'Who cares?' she thought. 'I don't suppose I'll be a bridesmaid ever again.'

6

Mattie and the Revels

Mattie belonged to the local Brownie pack. She hadn't wanted to join but her best friend Katie Kelly was a Brownie and she had wanted Mattie to be one too.

Mattie was in the Gnomes. The rhyme that the Gnomes had to sing made Mr and Mrs McCrum laugh in what Mattie considered to be a very rude way.

> *We are the happy Gnomes,*
> *Helping others in their homes.*

'That'll be the day,' said her father.

'I never heard such nonsense!' said Mrs McCrum.

Mattie felt she was a special Brownie because she was the only one in the whole pack without any badges. Katie Kelly had her Needlework and Pet Lover's badges and Angela Morris had so many badges you could hardly see her uniform.

'She's probably even got one for breathing,' said Mattie to Katie.

Brown Owl tried to make Mattie into the sort of Brownie she wanted her to be. Brown Owl found it VERY tiring.

'Well, these aren't QUITE right, dear,' she said when Mattie presented her with some dried up little clumps of mud which turned out to be rock buns.

Mattie tried to get her Pet Lover's Badge but her cat Stanley was not interested in helping her. He ran away at the sight of a brush, slept on top of the fridge, not in his warmly-lined basket, and only ate when he felt like it. He was always getting into fights with other cats so he never looked well groomed.

As for needlework! Mrs McCrum had to hold onto the table she was laughing so much when Mattie showed her the tea-cosy she had made. It was supposed to be in the shape of a grey mouse but Mrs McCrum thought it was a boat and Mattie was very offended. After that she gave up trying.

'Don't want any badges anyway,' she muttered.

'Wouldn't you like to try for your Gardening Badge, dear?' asked Brown Owl kindly. 'You could plant some nice little seeds and water them.'

Mattie didn't want to plant nice little anything. She had heard Mr McCrum say that nobody in his family had green fingers and all their gardens were like bomb sites.

She told this to Brown Owl who looked at Mattie with a wise, sad expression. 'Oh dear,' she said. 'I'm sure that's not true. I'm sure if you asked

Daddy to buy you some seeds and a little trowel you'd do very well.'

She did ask him and he said, 'If old Barn Owl wants to lay out good money on gardening tools for you then good luck to her but I've got better things to do with our money.'

So Mattie didn't say any more about it.

The next Saturday was the Brownie Revels. Brown Owl said this meant that they would have great fun playing with lots of other Brownies and singing round the camp fire.

'Singing,' thought Mattie. 'Oh help.'

On Saturday morning Mattie raced about trying to find her Brownie hat. She thought she had last used it for a doll's blanket . . . or for keeping her marbles in, but it wasn't in her room.

'How you can expect to find anything in this mess beats me,' said Mrs McCrum.

Everyone was hunting for the hat when Stanley the cat stood up on the fridge. He had been sleeping on the hat all night. Of course it was covered in bits of fluff and cat hairs so it had to be wiped with a wet cloth.

Mattie got to the Brownie hut just as the van was about to leave and Brown Owl was cross.

'I thought you'd rather have me late but in my proper uniform.' said Mattie.

'I suppose so,' said Brown Owl and patted her

head. 'My goodness . . . why is your hat all wet?'

Mattie was about to explain but Brown Owl just sighed and shoved her into the van where the other Brownies were waiting and giggling. Katie Kelly had saved her a place next to the window and gave her a pear drop so then Mattie didn't feel so bad.

On the journey Brown Owl made them sing, which of course Mattie was not happy about, because singing in public was one of her least favourite things.

'Sing up Mattie,' called Brown Owl from the driver's seat. 'I can't hear your voice.'

Angela Morris smirked and sang very loudly and clearly. So loudly and clearly, in fact, that Mattie could see her tonsils.

'Ugh,' she thought. 'Well, I wouldn't be so rude as to show everyone my tonsils. It's not a thing you want to see first thing in the morning.'

Angela had brought her bird-watching book, her camera, a magnifying glass and a small first-aid box. Mattie had brought four paperbacks, two blocks of chocolate, a new nightdress and a hair-slide shaped like a poodle.

'If anyone cuts themselves,' said Angela importantly, 'come to me if Brown Owl's not about because I've got PLENTY of plasters.'

'What if we break a leg ... or an arm?' Mattie asked her. 'I mean ... a plaster won't do for that. Still, I suppose you'll be able to make splints out of old branches and things.'

'Probably,' said Angela. 'I have got my First Aid Badge.'

Mattie didn't want to start Angela boasting about all her badges so she just sucked her pear drop loudly and stared out of the window.

'Nearly there, Brownies,' said Brown Owl. 'Don't get so excited that you feel sick.'

'If anyone does feel sick,' said Angela, 'you must breathe deeply . . . in and out . . . very slowly . . . and it should pass.'

Immediately, Mattie and Katie started to breathe in and out making a great deal of noise and sticking their tongues out as far as they would go.

'Bleeeeeaaaargh,' said Mattie.

'Yaaaaaaaaaark,' said Katie.

'Who on earth is making those TERRIBLE noises?' asked Brown Owl. 'And whoever it is . . . stop it.'

'Angela Morris told us to,' said Mattie innocently.

'Yes,' agreed Katie. 'She said that's what we must do if we felt sick.'

'And DO you feel sick?' asked Brown Owl.

'Oh no . . . not at all,' said Mattie. 'We were practising. Just in case.'

Angela Morris sulked for the rest of the journey.

When they arrived at the large field Brown Owl told Angela to divide the pack up into two teams.

'We're going to have a competition to see who can put their tent up fastest.'

Mattie hated teams. If it was sport or some-thing practical she was usually last to be picked because although she was popular she was not very enthusiastic about these things.

Angela blew a little whistle and looked self-important.

'Rally on me Brownies,' she called, and this made Mattie and Katie have a fit of giggles.

'Rally on me tent pegs,' whispered Mattie which made them giggle even more.

'I don't see what's funny,' said Angela. 'The trouble with you Mattie McCrum is, you've always got to turn everything into a joke.'

'It's only a tent,' said Mattie. 'It's not a matter of life and death.'

'Well, it easily could be,' said Angela. 'Suppose we didn't get the tents up and there was a storm and we had nowhere to shelter and it was pouring with rain. We could all end up with pneumonia and DIE!' she finished breathlessly.

'No we wouldn't,' said Mattie. 'We'd just shelter in the van.'

'Oh shut up,' Angela said crossly and she began sorting the Brownies into teams. Mattie was chosen last but her team won the competition and Brown Owl gave them all a boiled sweet each.

'You see dear,' she told Mattie. 'You can do it when you try.'

Mattie thought that perhaps she should tell her that all she'd done was give out the tent pegs, but Brown Owl was organising a camp fire, so she decided to keep quiet and let Brown Owl think well of her for a change.

To Mattie's amazement a large fire was soon blazing away. A very neat, well-organised fire.

'If I'd done that,' said Mattie to Katie, 'I bet the farm house would be on fire by now.'

Katie laughed. 'Where's your food?' she said as the other Brownies began to unpack tins of beans and sausages and sandwiches from their bags.

A feeling of panic ran through Mattie. How had all the others known to bring food with them?

'Didn't you give your Mum the note?' said Katie.

'Oh no! I forgot. Well, I didn't forget . . . I made a paper dart out of it and threw it at Angela. It hit her on the nose and she threw it away. I meant to get it at the end of Brownies but I forgot . . . at least I think I did . . .'

'Oh Mattie . . . you're HOPELESS,' said Katie, but not in a cross way. 'You'd better share mine . . . but I don't know what Brown Owl will say.'

'Or Angela,' said Mattie glumly.

'Come on girls,' shouted Brown Owl merrily.

'Oh dear,' said Katie. 'Here . . . hold this tin of beans and then it will look as though you've brought something.'

'No . . . it doesn't matter,' said Mattie. 'I've just had an idea. It might put me in Brown Owl's good books. Come on.'

Angela was busy giving out tin bowls and enamel mugs in a brisk and military manner.

'Anyone would think she was in an army camp,' thought Mattie. She could not resist running up to her, saluting like a soldier and saying, 'Private Mattie McCrum reporting for duty, sah!'

Angela ignored her and Brown Owl said, 'Why are you empty-handed, Mattie?'

'Well you see . . . I thought it would be a very good test of my skill as a Brownie if I didn't bring anything to eat and I had to go into woods and fields and forage for nourishment. Don't you think it's good idea?' Mattie said, trying to look eager and happy. 'I would like to prove that I'm not hopeless at everything. Please give me a chance Brown Owl. I'm sure I could find mushrooms and nettles and make a delicious little stew. Or something.' She finished lamely and Brown Owl looked at her. She DID want to give the child a chance. But all the same . . . she didn't really like the sound of it. She sighed.

'I suppose part of being a Brownie is learning how to think for yourself,' she said. 'Very well then, but you must not go far . . . you must not be longer than twenty minutes and you must come straight back here.'

Mattie grinned at Katie and Angela looked snooty as Mattie ran across the field.

'She needn't think that I'm going to eat any of her nettle stew,' mocked Angela.

Mattie climbed over the stile and felt very pleased with herself. It was nice to be alone and she walked along admiring the trees and the lovely view across the meadows. She began to hunt about but she couldn't see any mushrooms. Or even nettles. She found a very strange-looking plant with spotted, pale green leaves but it looked poisonous so she left it alone. Then she spent at least five minutes watching a furry caterpillar climb slowly over a leaf. She stroked its back with one finger but it curled itself up to get away from her.

She was convinced that a small hole in the grassy bank must be a fox lair and she peered into it. It was dark and she couldn't see much but she could hear an interesting scuffling noise from inside so she sat down to wait. Another ten minutes passed and nothing had happened. Nor had Mattie found any food.

'I'd better get on,' she told herself and she wandered along dreamily wishing she was a gypsy and could live in a horse-drawn caravan and sell pegs and paper flowers.

Mattie knew she would have to get back soon and she began to worry about not having found any food. It wasn't so much Brown Owl she was worried about as the superior look on Angela's face if she came back empty handed.

She busied herself hunting and hoping and she parted some long grass near the fence. To her surprise there was a little group of eggs on the ground. They were small, brown and speckled. Mattie couldn't think of any bird that laid eggs on the ground apart from a hen, but she knew these weren't hen's eggs. She decided somebody must have put them there and forgotten about them. What a lovely bit of luck! She wrapped them very carefully in her Brownie hat and walked back to the field.

Mattie could see Mr Cavendish, the farmer who had let them use his meadow to camp in. He was looking at her rather suspiciously but she gave what she hoped was a jolly, Brownie-ish sort of wave. He waved back but he didn't smile.

'Old cross-patch,' thought Mattie.

When she got back to the camp, most people had finished eating and Angela was building up the fire while the others cleared away.

'What are we having ... spider stew?' said Angela.

'No, ACTUALLY,' said Mattie.

She showed her the eggs in the hat. 'I'm not sure what to do with them though. Do you think they're all right to eat?'

Angela inspected them. 'Oh, 'course they are. You could make an omelette out of them.'

'Well ... I COULD,' said Mattie doubtfully. 'But I'm not sure what to do.'

'For goodness sake,' said Angela. 'Come here ... I'll do it for you.'

'Oh THANKS,' said Mattie happily. 'It's very kind of you.'

She had hoped all along that Angela would take charge and make the tea for her because she knew that Angela liked helping and liked being important. Neither of these two things held much appeal for Mattie.

In what seemed like seconds Angela had whisked the eggs with some milk and heated the frying pan. And in a few more seconds a delicious-looking omelette was sizzling.

'Oh Angela ... you ARE clever,' said Mattie, her mouth watering at the sight.

Just as Angela was about to scoop the omelette onto a plate Mattie heard a dreadful roaring sound. Everyone stared. It was Mr Cavendish, the farmer, and he was storming across the field towards them, shouting and waving his fist. Brown Owl, who had been demonstrating some new knots, looked rather alarmed.

'You,' he shouted at her. 'Mrs Owl or whatever you call yourself. I want a word.'

Mattie took her plate of omelette and began to gobble it up. If she was going to get into trouble, which somehow she felt she might, she wanted to be in trouble on a full stomach.

'One of your little brown NUISANCES,' roared Mr Cavendish. 'One of them has stolen my precious pheasant eggs. My valuable, rare and carefully nurtured pheasant's eggs. Gone. Stolen!'

'I'm terribly sorry,' said Brown Owl with her wise, kind look. 'I think there must have been a mistake. None of my Brownies are thieves you know. They all obey the Country Code most carefully. You won't find any pheasant's eggs here.'

'No ... and I know WHY I won't,' said Mr Cavendish. 'They're all in someone's stomach that's why. And I think I know who it might be.' He had seen Mattie quickly mopping up the last bit of egg with a piece of bread and Angela was scraping out the frying pan.

Mattie jumped up. It was do or die time. She knew she would have to confess. She cleared her throat and gave the Brownie salute.

'I Mattie McCrum,' she said, 'do admit that I unlawfully took some eggs and that they were cooked and that I ate them. I'm very sorry. I didn't know they were special eggs. They looked like any little eggs to me. They didn't really taste very special,' she added.

The whole Brownie pack groaned. 'Oh Mattie McCrum!'

Brown Owl groaned and so did Mr Cavendish.

Angela said, 'It can't be my fault. I didn't know. No one can blame me.'

Nobody seemed to know what to say. Brown Owl looked apologetic and wore her more-in-sorrow-than-in-anger look and Mr Cavendish stared ferociously at Mattie. She stared back. She was thinking, 'You can't frighten me with that stare ... it's only a stare. No one ever died from being stared at ... I'll just stare back.' This was to comfort herself because she did feel rather alarmed as Mr Cavendish looked so red and furious.

'Perhaps we could come to some arrangement,' said Brown Owl. 'We could pay you for the eggs.'

'Hah!' said Mr Cavendish. 'Money won't bring those eggs back.' He stalked away across the field

and Mattie thought, 'Now I'm for it. I wish I hadn't come.'

Katie gave her hand a little squeeze but that made Mattie feel worse. If she was upset and someone was very kind to her it always made her more tearful ... she blinked very hard and took Katie's hand away. Katie looked hurt.

Angela was saying to Brown Owl, 'I do hope you don't think I'm to blame. I just helped her to cook them that's all.'

'Be quiet Angela,' said Brown Owl, much to everyone's surprise. 'Mattie ... come here child and stop looking so hunted.'

'I feel hunted,' said Mattie. 'And I feel sick.'

'Now Brownies,' said Brown Owl, 'I want you all to listen to this. Mattie of course did a very wicked thing in stealing those eggs ...'

'I didn't STEAL them,' piped up Mattie. 'They were just THERE ...'

Brown Owl ignored her and carried on. She was talking in a quiet, important voice as though what she was telling them was something very special. Even Jessica and Sita who had been making daisy chains for each others' heads, stopped and listened.

'However ... she has more than made up for that by her good Brownie behaviour,' continued Brown Owl, much to Mattie's amazement.

She wondered if Brown Owl was getting her mixed up with somebody else. Or if she had heard wrong. She was so used to being in trouble and getting into messes and forgetting things that being praised in front of everyone made her feel a bit strange.

'Yes ... she did the hardest, most important thing of all. She didn't put the blame onto anybody else. She didn't try to wriggle out of it. She told the TRUTH. And I'm very proud of her.'

Mattie smirked and went pink.

'Even though she hasn't won any badges yet I'm going to give her a special badge for her behaviour today.' Brown Owl pinned a little gold star onto Mattie's tie.

All the Brownies clapped and Mattie pulled a silly face because she felt shy.

'You see dear . . . you have the makings of a fine Brownie in you after all,' Brown Owl told her.

Mattie felt she could have disagreed quite strongly over this last remark but she decided to keep to her usual rule which was, 'When in doubt, say nothing'.

She fingered her gold star, not really able to believe it was there.

Angela was looking rather sulky and saying to Jessica, 'Honestly, she gets away with everything. Fancy getting a gold star for being a thief.'

'I didn't,' shouted Mattie indignantly. 'I got it for telling the truth!'

Angela came up to Mattie and hissed, 'Teacher's pet,' at her, which Mattie thought was very unfair. If ever there was a girl who was teacher's pet it was Angela Morris. So Mattie stuck out her tongue even though she knew she ought to be forgiving and gracious.

Then Mattie went to find Katie. 'I'm sorry I wasn't nice before, I didn't mean it. But you know what it's like when you're upset.'

'Yes,' said Katie. 'Of course I do.'

That was the nice thing about Katie – she wasn't at all huffy like some girls would have been. They wandered back to the camp fire together and

Katie said, 'You're the luckiest person I ever met, Mattie.'

'Me?' cried Mattie in astonishment. 'What do you mean?'

'Because even when you're wrong, it all comes out right.'

Mattie didn't think this was quite true but she was pleased Katie thought she was lucky. It was much nicer than people feeling sorry for you.

'Well, I'm lucky to have you as a friend,' Mattie said loyally.

'Oh, don't start being soppy,' said Katie and they both laughed.

'Girls! Girls!' called Brown Owl. 'Do stop dawdling, we want to start the camp-fire songs.'

Mattie rolled her eyes.

'If she asks me to sing by myself I'll refuse. Even if it means losing the only badge I've ever had.'

'Oh Mattie,' said Katie. 'That's JUST like you!'